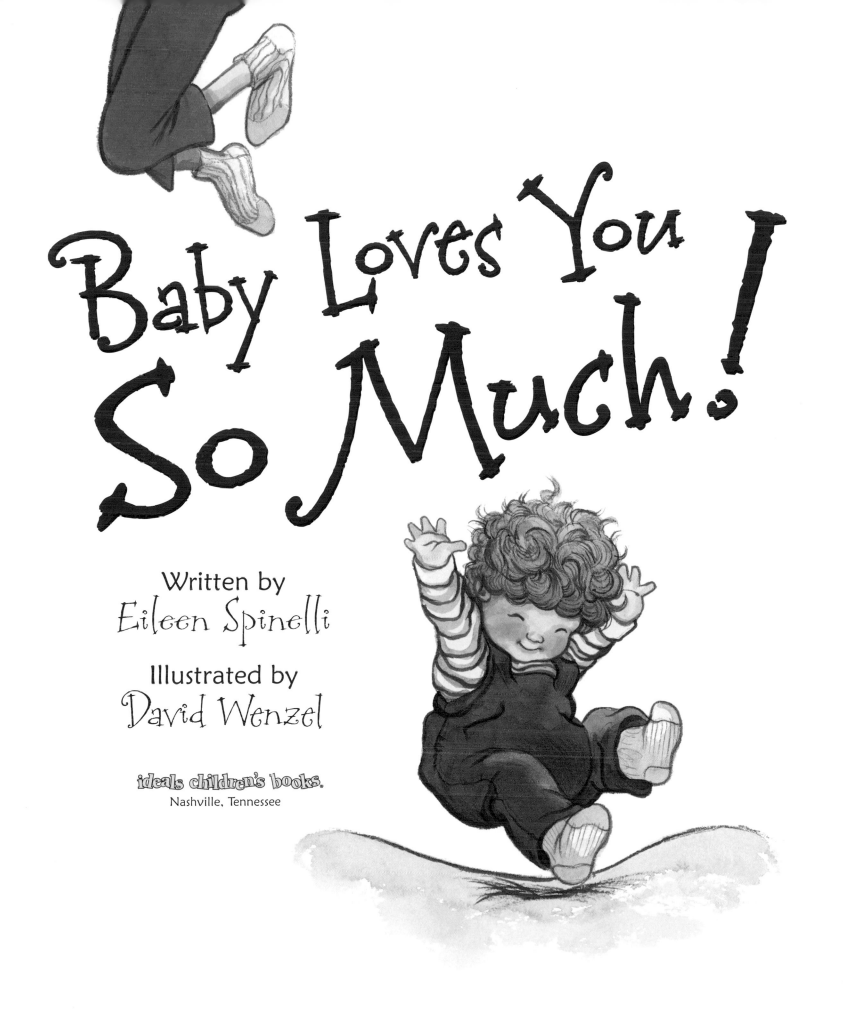

Baby Loves You So Much!

Written by
Eileen Spinelli

Illustrated by
David Wenzel

ideals children's books.
Nashville, Tennessee

ISBN 13: 978-0-8249-5550-2
ISBN 10: 0-8249-5550-1

Published by Ideals Children's Books
An imprint of Ideals Publications
A Guideposts Company
535 Metroplex Drive, Suite 250
Nashville, Tennessee 37211
www.idealsbooks.com

Color separations by Precision Color Graphics, Franklin, Wisconsin

Printed and bound in Italy by LEGO

Library of Congress Cataloging-in-Publication Data

Spinelli, Eileen.
  Baby loves you so much! / written by Eileen Spinelli ; illustrated by
David Wenzel.
    p. cm.
  Summary: Even though her baby brother annoys her by slobbering
on her homework and hitting her on the head with his ball, a big sister
realizes that she loves him very much.
  ISBN-13: 978-0-8249-5550-2 (alk. paper)
  ISBN-10: 0-8249-5550-1 (alk. paper)
  [1. Babies—Fiction. 2. Brothers and sisters—Fiction.]   I. Wenzel,
David, date   , ill. II. Title.
PZ7.S7566Bab 2006
[E]—dc22
                                              2006027734

10 9 8 7 6 5 4 3 2 1

Designed by Eve DeGrie

To Jeanne and Bill Twining
Faythe and Bob Captain
Eleanore Dower —*E.S.*

To Lindsey —*D.W.*

"Baby loves you so much!"

That's what Mom says when Baby
wakes me up in the morning
screaming . . .

Waaaaa! Waaaaa!

"Baby wants you to be awake too,"
says Mom. "To enjoy this bright
new day."

Great. A baby brother
who thinks he's an alarm clock.

"Baby loves you so much!"

That's what Mom says when Baby spatters me with oatmeal.

Splat! Splat! Splat!

"Baby wants to share his breakfast," says Mom.

Oh, no—here come the diced peaches!

"Baby loves you so much!"

That's what Mom says when Baby
pulls my hair.
Yank! Yank!
"Baby just wants you to come closer,"
says Mom. "Maybe he has a secret to tell you."

And maybe I'm going to be bald before
I'm ten.

"Baby loves you so much!"

That's what Mom says when Baby
bites my finger with his four front teeth.
Chomp! Chomp! Chomp!
"Baby thinks you taste really sweet,"
says Mom.

Will somebody please give this baby
a chocolate cookie?

"Baby loves you so much!"

That's what Mom says when Baby
grabs three of my puzzle pieces.
Giggle. Giggle.
"Baby wants to help you put
your puzzle together," says Mom.

In the cat's water dish?

"Baby loves you so much!"

That's what Mom says when Baby
pops me in the nose.
Smack. Smack. Smack.
"Baby's trying to teach you
pat-a-cake," says Mom.

I already know pat-a-cake—
There are no noses involved.

"Baby loves you so much!"

That's what Mom says when Baby
throws his ball at my head.
Boink! Boink!
"Baby wants you to be his basketball
coach," says Mom.

Memo to Baby: Bopping your coach on
the head will get you a seat on the bench.

"Baby loves you so much!"

That's what Mom says when Baby
slobbers on my long-division paper.
Slurple . . . slurple . . .
"Baby's eager to help you with
your homework," says Mom.

Wonderful. Tell that to my math teacher,
Miss Hathaway.

Baby
is very,
very
quiet.

No screaming.
No giggling.
No boinking.
Where is Baby?

Not crawling on the kitchen floor.
Not toddling around the hall.
Not climbing on the sofa.

I start to worry.

Baby! Baby!
Where are you?

At last
I see—
curly blonde hair . . .
blue overalls . . .
little green socks . . .

It's Baby
under the dining-room table,
sound asleep.
Zaaaaaaaa.
Baby's soft snoring
makes me smile . . .
makes me realize
I'm sleepy too.

I snuggle next to Baby . . .
close my eyes . . .
whisper in Baby's ear,

"Big sister loves you so much!"

About the Author

Eileen Spinelli began writing stories as a child in Upper Darby, Pennsylvania, when her father gave her an old manual typewriter. Today, she still loves writing. She says she is so eager to start writing each morning that she just runs "upstairs in my nightie, with a cup of tea and an idea or two." She still lives in Pennsylvania, with her husband, Jerry, and loves having her many grandchildren visit.

About the Artist

David Wenzel paints his whimsical watercolors in his hilltop studio that overlooks a meadow with a meandering stream. When not painting, Wenzel enjoys playing the guitar or presenting art workshops for schools. He lives in Connecticut with his wife, their two sons, and Gus, their grumpy pot-bellied pig.